SBN: # 978-1-7366074-1-1
Text Copyright © 2022 by Mynecia Steele
Illustration Copyright © 2022 by Mynecia Steele

This is a work of fiction. Names, characters, places, and incidents either are the products of the author's imagination or are used fictitiously. Any resemblance to actual persons, living or dead, businesses, companies, events, or locales is entirely coincidental.

For permission requests, please contact the author via email at: mynebymynecia@gmail.com

Proudly self-published through Divine Legacy Publishing, www.divinelegacypublishir

D1160339

DEDICATION

I would like to thank every teacher, community member, and even the random social media followers who have encouraged me to continue drawing.

A special thanks goes to my family and my closest friends.

Thank you all for influencing the world that is my imagination. Thank you for all the 'good jobs' over the years, even when I may not have done such a good job. I love you all for loving me enough to give me honest feedback over the years.

Thank you, thank you, thank you!

PICTURE THAT

Written & Illustrated By:

MYNECIA STEELE

When I was little,
my family would have drawing contests.

1

Daddy would spread out a ginormous piece of paper. Mommy would always find markers and crayons in every color of the rainbow. My big sister would get the snacks, usually peanut butter and jelly. That's her favorite! I was in charge of pencils. After all, I was the best artist in the family. And everyone knows artists have a lot of pencils.

2

Mommy would cover her eyes and let us pick something in the room for her to draw. Daddy could find the funniest objects, like lint or pennies from under the couch. Daddy was also an expert at drawing old cartoons that I had never heard of, but they always turned out like the picture on his phone. My sister drew really pretty flowers and fruit baskets. I liked to draw people.

One day, everyone else started being busy— all of the time.

But, me?
I kept on drawing!

Mommy had to watch the new baby. I wasn't jealous or anything. He was so cute! I could look at him all day, too. Sometimes, I did.

Mommy loved the pictures I drew of him.
"Wow, you must be the greatest artist in the whole wide world!"
Mommy said.

When mommy and the baby were napping, I liked to watch my big sister have fashion shows. I would pretend to be a fashion designer. She told me that my drawings looked better than any of her clothes. "I can't wait to wear clothes with your name on the tags," she said.

Some days, I would go to work with daddy. His clients would ask for pictures in their hair. Daddy said the clippers were too sharp for me to try. So, I drew his customers instead. Some of them would even buy my pictures for 5¢.

One day at school, my teacher told us we could dress up for career day. I knew just what to be—an artist! Mommy helped me decorate an apron with paint, like a real artist. I picked out my favorite pencil

9   and some of my favorite drawings to show my class.

When it was my turn, I was so excited.
"My name is Mya S," I said loud, just
like Daddy and me practiced.
"When I grow up, I will be an artist!"
I yelled even more proudly.

10

I held up my pictures. But, instead of saying "wow," one of the kids pointed at me. She laughed and said, "Ugh! What is that?"

I was so sad walking home. "What's raining on your day, my sweet baby?" Mommy asked. "All of you told me a story," I said in my grumpiest voice. "I don't understand. You don't have any sad storybooks," Mommy said with a caring, yet confused face. "Not that kind of story! A not-true!" I said running into the house.

12

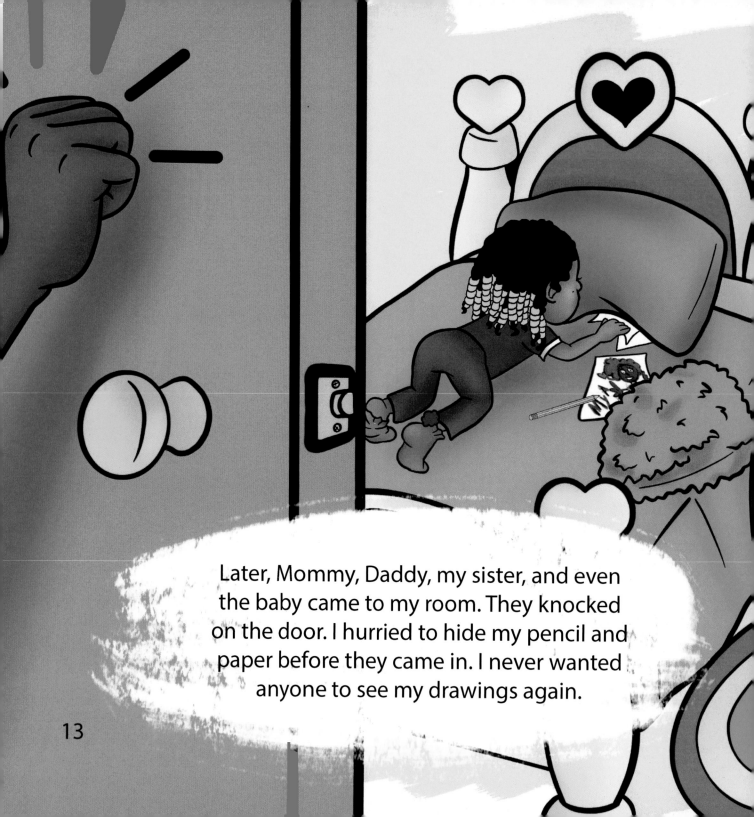

Later, Mommy, Daddy, my sister, and even the baby came to my room. They knocked on the door. I hurried to hide my pencil and paper before they came in. I never wanted anyone to see my drawings again.

Mommy talked first. "Sugar lump, I called your teacher," she started, rubbing my knee. "She told me what happened today, honey poo." I peeked from behind my pillow.

"There she is," Daddy cut in. "Do you remember why you wanted to dress up like an artist?" "I don't know," I said. Then, I remembered why. So, I added, "Because drawing is fun. I thought people liked looking at my pictures, but those kids didn't."

"Well, did you know that I wasn't always good at cutting hair?" Daddy asked.

I shook my head.

"I was not!" Daddy said laughing.

Then, he pulled a picture of his brother from his pocket. There was a big piece of hair missing from the middle of my uncle's head. "Can you believe that even after that your uncle still let me practice on him? We laughed so hard that day, but he said that he could see the talent in me. And, even more than that, he could tell that I really loved cutting hair."

16

"Speaking of fails," my sister said, moving closer to me.
"I wasn't always a fashionista."
"What do you mean?" I asked. "You said you have lots of followers,
and people always like your pictures."
"Yeah, a lot of people like my new pictures, but that's not why I post.
The truth is that fashion is my favorite thing."

She started sliding her finger
really fast on her phone.

Finally, she pointed her phone
to my face.

"This was my first post," she said.
"No one has ever liked it
except me and—it's okay."

"What we're trying to say baby cakes, is we will always support whatever makes you happy," Mommy said in her softest voice. "It's important to do what makes you happy."
"Being a mommy is my favorite thing in the world. And, maybe I didn't do a good job when I told you a 'not-true,' but that is not going to make me stop being a mommy."

"So, you think my drawings are bad?"
"I think your drawings are amazing!"
I turned my head sideways,
wondering what she would say next.
"But, just maybe, they aren't the greatest
artwork in the whole wide world."

"You know what? The girl at school sure likes to laugh," I said feeling much better. "Maybe she should be a comedian." Mommy shrugged her shoulders and nodded.

"Mommy, I should have known that I wasn't the most greatest artist in the whole wide world," I said. "Daddy told me you hadn't seen the WHOLE world." Mommy nudged Daddy's arm.

21

"Or, maybe you should
be the comedian!" my sister
chuckled and told me.

"Because that was hilarious.
I'm definitely posting that."

"No thanks," I said
standing on my fuzzy pillow.

I held up my drawing and
shouted, "I'm an artist!"

Then, my lil brother made a
goo-goo sound, but I knew
what he was trying to say was
'keep drawing sis!'

MEET THE
AUTHOR

2006   2016   2018   2020   2022

Mynecia (Mya) Steele is a native of Eutaw, Alabama. Growing up in a small town, her favorite childhood memories like drawing with her sister and parents, were made right in her own home. Born to a barber and a baker, creativity was in her bones. She is a proud graduate of Troy University, where she earned her degree in journalism and minored in graphic design. Mynecia has illustrated dozens of books, and she is excited to release her first book as an author!

Made in the USA
Columbia, SC
30 March 2022